The Deluxe Junior Novelization

rhcbooks.com

ISBN 978-0-525-58070-6 (hc) — ISBN 978-0-525-58071-3 (ebook)

Printed in the United States of America

10 9 8 7 6 5 4 3 2 1

JURASSIC PARK
25TH ANNIVERSARY

The Deluxe Junior Novelization

Adapted by Gail Herman

From a screenplay by Michael Crichton and David Koepp

Based on the novel by Michael Crichton

Random House 🏠 New York

PROLOGUE

On a small island off the coast of South America, nighttime fell. Searchlights clicked on. Suddenly, a tropical jungle was brightly lit. A dozen workers stood guard around a section of the jungle. The area was closed off by a tall electrified fence—the kind of fence that would surround a prison. But this wasn't a prison. It was an animal pen.

The workers got their stun guns ready. Slowly, a large crate was lowered to the ground. A door slid open in the fence. Then the crate was pushed up against the opening, and a worker jumped on top of it. He grabbed hold of the handles, trying to lift a panel. It was stuck. The worker pulled harder. Then, all at once, the panel flew up and the worker lost his balance. He fell to the ground on the other side of the fence.

And the crate was open.

Roar! A terrifying sound came from inside. Quick as lightning, a claw whipped out. It reached for the fallen worker. Then it took hold and dragged him toward the crate.

"Fire! Fire! Now!" ordered a voice. The stun guns flashed. But it was too late. The worker was gone.

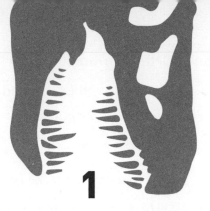

1

The sun beat down on Dr. Alan Grant. It was hot, and there were no trees to give him shade. There was just the dust and rocks of the Montana Badlands. But Alan Grant was a paleontologist on an archaeological dig. He didn't care about the heat. He didn't care how scruffy he looked with his stubbly chin and dusty clothes. He was interested in only one thing—dinosaurs.

Alan bent closer to the ground. He was looking at a dinosaur fossil.

"Four complete skeletons in such a small area," he said to Dr. Ellie Sattler. "These Raptors probably hunted as a team. The Tenontosaurus bones over there must have been left over from lunch."

Ellie, a slim, blond woman, leaned closer to the fossil. She studied the bones, too.

"Dr. Grant! Dr. Sattler!" called a volunteer from across the dig. "We're ready to try the computer again."

Alan sighed. He didn't want to leave the excavation site. "I hate computers," he muttered to Ellie as they headed back to the base camp. Alan didn't care for the camp, either. It was like a circus, with tents everywhere and grown-ups and kids running around.

"Why do these volunteers have to bring their kids, anyway?" Alan asked.

Ellie didn't answer. She knew how Alan felt about kids. For some reason, he just didn't like them.

Alan and Ellie walked into one of the tents. Inside, volunteers were grouped around a computer screen. They were looking at a dinosaur skeleton. A radar pellet had been shot into the ground around the fossils. They could see the entire skeleton without digging it up.

"Velociraptor?" Ellie asked Alan.

"Yes. Good shape, too. Look at the bone in the wrist. No wonder dinosaurs learned to fly."

A volunteer laughed. "Dinosaurs? Fly?"

"Obviously, you haven't read my book," Alan said to him. "Maybe dinosaurs have more in common with birds than reptiles. Even the word *Raptor*—as in Velociraptor—means 'bird of prey.'"

A boy stepped forward to look at the screen. "It doesn't look very scary," he said. "It looks more like a six-foot turkey!"

Alan looked the boy over. "Not scary, huh? Try to imagine yourself in the age of dinosaurs. You move into a clearing. But the Raptor knew you were there a long time ago. It bobs its head and moves like a bird. You keep still. You think if you don't move, he won't see you. That would work with the Tyrannosaurus rex. But not the Velociraptor. The attack comes. Not from the front. Not from the side. It comes from two Raptors you didn't even know were there. They slash at you with their claws. It's like a razor cut. Fast and deep."

The boy backed away, his eyes wide with fear. "So try and show a little respect," Alan said as he left the tent.

Ellie came up behind him. "If you wanted to scare him, you could have just pulled a gun."

Alan shrugged. He felt a little bad, but he just didn't like kids. They were always in the way. "You know," he said, "me and kids . . ."

"You old fossil!" Ellie said, giving him a hug.

Ellie loved Alan. But he could be so annoying—especially when it came to kids. She wondered if he would ever change. If not, could they have a future together?

Suddenly, a strong wind sprang up. Dirt and sand blew everywhere, and a roaring noise filled the air. A helicopter was landing.

An elderly man got out of the helicopter. Alan was furious. Who was this man? Why had he flown in like that? Didn't he realize there was a dig going on?

But before Alan had a chance to say anything, the man introduced himself.

"John Hammond," he said. "It's nice to finally meet you, Dr. Grant."

John Hammond! The name sank in, and Alan realized he was talking to the man who was funding the excavation.

"I can see my money has been well spent," Mr. Hammond continued, looking around. "But I'll get right to the point. I own an island off the coast of South America. I spent the last five years setting up an animal preserve there. It's really fantastic. Our attractions will send kids right out of their minds. But there's this lawyer. He says I need experts to look over the park. I'd like you two to give your okay. You know, say that it's safe. Endorse it. I'd like you to come down for the weekend. I already have a jet waiting."

"What kind of park is it?" asked Alan.

"It's . . ." John Hammond paused, smiling. "Right up your alley."

Dennis Nedry sat at an outdoor table in a restaurant, waiting impatiently. He was a large man with a big grin. But his eyes were cold and the grin was nasty. Very nasty.

Nedry watched as a taxi pulled up to the curb and a man carrying a briefcase got out. "Over here, Dodgson," Nedry called to him, still grinning.

Dodgson headed over, then slid his briefcase across the table. "You shouldn't use my name," he whispered.

"Dodgson, Dodgson, Dodgson," Nedry said even louder as he took the briefcase. Nedry didn't care if he made Dodgson mad. He only cared about the money he was going to make. Dodgson's company wanted something Mr. Hammond already had: dinosaur specimens. They wanted to clone dinosaurs, too. And as the designer of Hammond's high-tech security system, Dennis Nedry could help them. For a price, of course.

Dodgson pointed to the briefcase. "There's seven hundred and fifty thousand dollars in there," he said. "You'll get the rest on delivery. That's fifty thousand for each specimen. And there are fifteen of them."

Nedry's eyes narrowed. "I know, I know. Don't worry. I'll get them all. How do I carry them off the island?"

Dodgson showed him an ordinary can of shaving cream. Then he slid the bottom open. Inside were fifteen different compartments—one for each specimen.

Nedry nodded his approval. "I'll meet your guy tomorrow night at the dock. Make sure he gets it right. I built eighteen minutes into the computer program so I can beat the security system. Eighteen minutes and your company gets years' worth of research."

"Shh," Dodgson said hurriedly. A waiter was coming over to leave the check. Nedry looked down at it, then up at Dodgson, smiling his nasty grin.

Dodgson paid the check.

A few hours later Ellie and Alan were in South America. They were boarding a helicopter that would take them to Mr. Hammond's island. Besides Mr. Hammond, there were two other men with them. The first was a lawyer Mr. Hammond had told them about, Donald Gennaro. He seemed nervous. And even though he was wearing a safari outfit, he still looked like he'd be more comfortable sitting behind a desk.

The other passenger was Dr. Ian Malcolm. Ian Malcolm was a mathematician. Like Alan and Ellie, he was going to check over the park. Tall, thin, and dressed all in black, he also looked out of place. But he didn't seem nervous. Instead, it seemed as if Ian found the whole situation funny.

"This park won't work," he was saying to Mr. Hammond, "because of chaos theory. In the end, everything is unpredictable."

Alan and Ellie didn't know what he was talking

about. They weren't even sure what the park was about. So they kept quiet.

Minutes later, the island rose sharply out of the water. Thick clouds covered its sheer cliffs. It looked strange and mysterious—like it belonged to another time.

"Hold on," said Mr. Hammond. "We're going to land and it may be a little rough."

Suddenly the helicopter dropped like a stone. Then it hit the ground with a jolt. Mr. Hammond waved grandly as he opened the helicopter door.

"Welcome to Jurassic Park!"

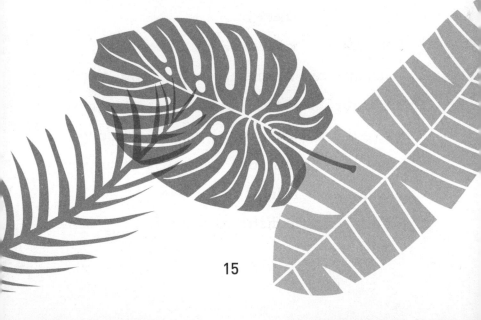

2

Everyone piled into two waiting trucks. In one, Mr. Hammond was talking to Donald Gennaro. "Relax and enjoy yourself. It's completely safe here. All the fences are electrified, and the full fifty miles of it are in place."

Slowly the vehicles wound their way along mountain roads. The island was lush with greenery. Ellie, in the other vehicle, craned her neck to look at the tropical plant life. Something seemed odd to her. She reached out for a leafy branch. As the truck drove along, she tore it off.

This plant shouldn't be here, she thought. It's extinct.

The vehicles bounced down a narrow path, then stopped at the side of a moat. Alan twisted in his seat to look around. There were some very strange trees here. They didn't have any leaves. Alan raised his head, looking higher . . . and higher still. Suddenly his mouth dropped in surprise. Those weren't tree trunks at all. They were legs. He lifted his head back all the way. And the legs belonged to a dinosaur! A living, breathing dinosaur.

"Oh!" said Ellie, seeing it, too. The Brachiosaurus, thirty-five feet tall, stared down at the people in the trucks.

Mr. Hammond strolled over to their truck, smiling happily. He looked like a kid showing off his new bicycle. "You want to pet it?" he asked.

No one could answer. The sight of the giant dinosaur was too much. Ian Malcolm just stared in amazement. Then he said, "You did it! You actually did it!"

Alan still couldn't speak. He could only stand in his

seat, trying to get closer to the Brachiosaurus. Then he noticed the other dinosaurs. There was a whole group of them across the moat, munching on leaves from the treetops.

He let out a whoop of joy. "Ha!" he cried as Gennaro came running over.

"Are these, are these, are—" Gennaro stuttered.

"They're herbivores," Mr. Hammond said. "Relax—they only eat plants!"

Gennaro seemed to calm down, but Ian Malcolm couldn't resist teasing him a little. "It could still step on you," he said smugly.

Finally, Alan and Ellie found the words they were looking for. They both began to talk at the same time.

"The movement, the grace—it's not what—" Alan said.

"—the experts said," Ellie continued. "We can just—"

"—tear up the rule book," Alan finished for her. In the distance, a herd of dinosaurs ran across a grassy plain. "Look," he said. "They move—"

"—in herds!" said Ellie. "We were right!"

Now everyone was chattering excitedly. But the Brachiosaurus didn't take any notice. It had a dull, pleasant expression on its face. And as it stretched its long neck across the moat and passed right in front of the truck, its expression didn't change.

Gennaro drew back in alarm. But the dinosaur was just reaching for some nearby leaves. A moment later, the dinosaur pulled back, dropping branches on the hood like a dribbling baby.

Mr. Hammond led Gennaro back to the first vehicle. The cars started up again and everyone kept talking as they drove through the park. "The dinosaurs are amazing!" said Alan and Ellie. "The park will be a wild success!" said Gennaro. All his fears were forgotten. They were going to make millions!

The only one who kept quiet was Ian Malcolm. As the vehicles pulled into the main compound, he said one word: "Crazy!" And he shook his head in dismay.

The main compound was a large area fenced in from the rest of the park. Inside were three structures. Walkways led from one structure to another, and workers bustled all around. They were completing the buildings—finishing walls, placing bars in the windows. There was still a lot to do. Only one structure was complete. And it wasn't even a building. It looked more like an animal pen—or a prison.

Mr. Hammond took everyone to the biggest building. It was the Visitor's Center. In the lobby, two huge skeletons were under construction: a Tyrannosaurus rex and a Brachiosaurus. As the group walked past the scaffolding, Hammond started to explain the park.

"It will be the biggest, best amusement park in the world. I'm not just talking about rides. We made living, breathing attractions so astonishing, they'll capture everyone's attention. Now, I bet you're wondering how these dinosaurs got here. Well, it's all part of the miracle of cloning. We made the dinosaurs from blood samples!"

"Where do you get one-hundred-million-year-old dinosaur blood?" asked Ellie.

"You'll see," said Mr. Hammond, leading everyone into a theater.

The lights dimmed as everyone took a seat. Then a film came on the screen. A cartoon character that looked like two pieces of rope twisted together popped into view.

"I'm Mr. DNA. I come from your blood. Your blood has billions of DNA strands. A strand like me is a plan for building a living thing. I'm a blueprint for how something grows.

"Now, a long time ago there were mosquitoes, just like there are today. And just like today they fed on animal blood. Dinosaur blood! Sometimes a mosquito would bite a dinosaur. Then it would land on a tree and get stuck in the sap. After a long time, the tree sap would get hard and turn into a fossil—just like dinosaur bones turn into fossils. This fossil, called amber, would keep the mosquito exactly the way it was when it bit the dinosaur.

"Then the amber waited for millions of years until Jurassic Park scientists came along. They took the blood from the mosquito. And—bingo! They got dino DNA! But there were pieces missing. So the scientists filled the gaps with frog DNA. Why? Because it's so similar! Then they put the DNA into an empty ostrich egg. Pretty soon they got a baby dinosaur!"

Suddenly bars came down on the seats and the chairs began to move. Alan and the others were taken through automatic doors into a laboratory. The room was bathed in a strange glow—an ultraviolet light that covered dozens of ostrich eggs. Quickly, Alan lifted the bar on his seat. He ran over to a table. One of the eggs cracked open. A tiny dinosaur head popped out.

"Look!" said Alan. The others rushed over.

Mr. Hammond smiled. "I like being here for the birth of every dinosaur," he said.

"But you can't be," Ian put in. "What about the dinosaurs born in the wild?"

"Oh, that can't happen," Mr. Hammond answered. "You see, all the dinosaurs are female."

Ian didn't believe him. "How do you know? Do you go into the park and . . . uh . . . lift their skirts? Because you can't control something like that. Life cannot be controlled. It breaks free. It grows. Life always finds a way."

Alan, meanwhile, was holding the baby dinosaur. It looked like a yellow lizard with brown stripes. Alan measured and weighed it with lab equipment. He counted the bones running along its back. It can't be that kind of dinosaur, he thought. No one would take that kind of chance.

"What species is this?" he asked.

"It's a Velociraptor," said Mr. Hammond.

"You breed *Raptors*?" said Alan. His voice trembled just a bit.

3

The Raptors were kept in the animal pen right in the compound. Alan rushed over, the others following behind.

"We planned to show you the Raptors after lunch," Mr. Hammond said, trying to lead Alan back to the Visitor's Center.

But Alan was intent on seeing the dinosaurs. He leaned in close to the fence, making sure not to touch it. He didn't see any Raptors. The pen was too overgrown with jungle plants and trees. But Alan did see a giant crane. It was dropping a large animal into the pen. Alan squinted. It looked like a steer.

The steer seemed frightened. Its legs were still attached to the crane by a thick rope. They flailed wildly as it fell. Then the animal disappeared behind some trees and the rope went slack.

Suddenly the rope jerked, like a fishing rod that had just caught a fish. Then it twisted and turned every which way. Plants shook back and forth. Alan heard vicious growls and a crunching sound. Seconds later, all was quiet.

The crane pulled up the rope. There was nothing on the end. The steer was gone. Every bit of it had been eaten.

Everyone stood in silence. They were too shocked to speak.

"The Raptors," said a grim voice. "They should all be destroyed."

Robert Muldoon, the park's game warden, was standing behind them. He had a hard look on his face.

"They're killers at eight months old," he continued. "They move at cheetah speed—sixty miles an hour.

And they're amazing jumpers."

"Are they intelligent?" asked Alan.

"Very."

Mr. Hammond clapped his hands together. He wanted everyone's attention. "Yes, but we've taken steps for safety," he said. "We have the electrical fence. We'll have steel frames on all the windows. Everything is under control. Now, who's hungry?"

Lunch was served in the Visitor's Center restaurant. Afterward, everyone stayed at the table. They were talking about the park.

"We're going to make a fortune," Gennaro said happily. "And we can charge anything we want!" His earlier fears had been replaced by greed.

Mr. Hammond frowned at him. That wasn't why he built the park. He built it for dinosaur lovers. For children. Eagerly, he listened to the others.

"Don't you see the danger?" Ian Malcolm was

saying. "You've used scientific power like a child who found his father's gun. You don't know what you've created."

Then Ellie spoke up. "The question is, how much can you know about an extinct system?"

Mr. Hammond looked upset. Two experts thought the park would fail. And Alan, after thinking long and hard, had to agree. Dinosaurs and humans—together! No one knew what would happen!

Outside a horn blasted. Mr. Hammond stood up and said, "You four are going to have a little company when you visit the park." He was hoping a Jurassic Park tour would change their minds. "Maybe Tim and Alexis will help you get into the spirit!"

"Who?" said Alan.

Mr. Hammond ushered his grandchildren into the room. Tim looked like he was about nine years old. His sister, Alexis, looked about twelve. "After all," said Mr. Hammond, introducing them all, "kids are our real audience."

Kids here, too? Alan thought. He'd never escape them.

⇀ ⇀ ⇀ ⇀

Two electric cars pulled up in front of the Visitor's Center. They were running along a rail, almost like a train.

"I read your book," Tim said to Alan as they waited to board. He was looking at the paleontologist with wide eyes. Tim was a dinosaur nut, and Dr. Alan Grant was his hero. "Do you really think dinosaurs turned into birds?"

"Well, uh, a few species may have evolved . . . ," Alan stammered. For some reason, this kid was making him nervous. He tried to move away, but Tim kept on his heels. Alan walked around and around the two cars, trying to lose him. Finally everyone settled into the cars' seats. Alan relaxed. Tim sat with Alexis and Gennaro in the front car. Alan was in the second one with Ellie and Ian Malcolm.

"We'll be watching from the control room," Mr. Hammond said to them.

The cars jerked forward. They passed through big iron gates. Seconds later, they were in the jungle.

A voice came over the speakers in both cars.

"Welcome to Jurassic Park," it said.

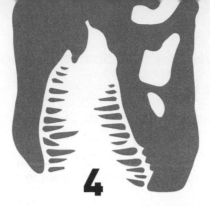

4

Inside the first car, Gennaro hit the buttons on a video display. "What's wrong with this computer?" he muttered. "I can't make it work."

"It's an interactive CD-ROM," Alexis explained. She took over the controls.

"Lex is a computer nerd," Tim said.

Lex corrected him. "I'm a hacker."

Just then the cars came to a stop. They were on top of a hill. Below them was a field with a river running through it.

"Look to your right," the recorded voice was saying. "You will see a herd of dinosaurs called

Dilophosaurus. This carnivore—or meat-eater—is poisonous. The Dilophosaurus spits venom, which blinds and paralyzes the prey so that it can't see or move."

The passengers pressed up against the car windows. They heard a faint hooting sound, but they didn't see a single dinosaur. After a few frustrating moments, the cars started up again and moved along a high ridge. At last they stopped at the edge of a large, open plain. A tall fence stood in front of the cars, and danger signs were posted all around.

The cars were right next to the Tyrannosaur paddock. Once again, everyone squirmed in their seats for a better look. But there was nothing. No Tyrannosaurus rex. They sat back, disappointed.

Ian picked up a microphone that connected him to the control room.

"You do plan to have dinosaurs on this dinosaur tour, right?" he asked Mr. Hammond.

Alan stared out the window. He thought he saw . . .

There! At the far end of the field, outside the fence—he saw something. But the cars were moving again. Alan had to see what it was. He pushed open the door and jumped out.

"Alan?" Ellie said, surprised. She jumped out, too.

"That's chaos theory in action," Ian muttered to himself. "Nobody could have predicted they'd jump out of a moving vehicle." Then he left the car.

Soon everybody was out in the open, following Alan Grant down the hill.

Back in the control room, Mr. Hammond was watching everything on video screens. There were dozens of screens set up around the room. They showed different parts of the park—and all the different dinosaurs.

There were computer terminals, too. They worked the video screens and kept the phones in order, the fences electrified, and all the security systems operating. They controlled Jurassic Park. They also made the room look like mission control for a space launch.

But the control room wasn't finished yet. People were bustling about, making sure everything worked. Ladders were scattered here and there. And cables were still lying around. Muldoon pushed one aside as he made his way over to Mr. Hammond.

"National Weather Service says a storm is heading this way," he said. "It could be dangerous. We'll have to stop the tour."

Ray Arnold, the head technician, shook his head with worry. He leaned over to look at the screen with Mr. Hammond. Then he jotted down some notes.

"Headlights broken," he said, looking at the electric cars. "This computer's not on its feet yet."

"Dennis!" Mr. Hammond called out to Dennis Nedry, the computer expert. "These lives are in your hands." Then his eyes widened in shock. Alan and the others were leaving the cars!

Dennis Nedry wasn't interested in the tour group. Or in the problems with the computer system. It was time to execute his plan to steal the dinosaur specimens for Dodgson. On his computer screen, he called up a picture of a supply ship by a dock. The ship was pitching back and forth on rough waters. Then Nedry pressed another button and the screen changed. Now it showed a steel door marked RESTRICTED. Nedry knew dinosaur specimens were kept behind that door.

Nedry went over his plan in his head: Shut down the security system. Put the dinosaur specimens in the fake shaving can. Then drive to the dock and hand them over to the ship worker. That was all he had to do. The ship worker would take the specimens to Dodgson on the mainland. Then Dodgson would pay him the rest of the money, and Nedry would be a rich man!

Nedry picked up the phone and called the ship.

"We have to leave," the sailor told him. "The storm is coming."

"I'll be there in fifteen minutes," Nedry said. He knew he should wait for Alan and the others to get back. They could have trouble when the security system went off. But Nedry didn't have time. And the money was too important to him. He turned back to the computer. Making sure no one was looking, Nedry entered a series of commands. A red box appeared. Inside it was one word: EXECUTE.

The skies over Jurassic Park had grown dark. The storm was coming closer.

"Uh, anybody think we shouldn't be out here?" Gennaro said. He looked to the right, then to the left. He hoped there weren't any dinosaurs out here.

But Alan knew something *was* out here. And he wanted to investigate. He kept going down the hill, and the others followed. Lex, though, wasn't looking where she was going. She stumbled on a loose rock. Alan grabbed her hand, stopping her from a fall. Lex smiled up at him. And when he tried to let go, she held tight.

Suddenly, the group stopped in its tracks. There it

was! A Triceratops, lying on its side. Its big frill circled its head like a bonnet. Tim stared at its three horns—one above each eye and one on the end of its nose. He grinned.

"I'm scared," said Lex.

Tim wasn't. He ran up to the dinosaur, with Alan right behind. Poor Trike, thought Alan. It's barely moving.

Next to the Triceratops crouched Dr. Gerry Harding. Dr. Harding was the animal caretaker for the park. He was examining the dinosaur.

"It's okay," he said, gesturing everyone else over, too. "She's been tranquilized. She seems to get sick like this every six weeks. We can't figure out what's wrong."

Alan bent close to the dinosaur. Its dark-purple tongue hung limply from its mouth. "Ellie, look at this," he said.

Ellie examined the tongue. Then she took a penlight and shined it in the Triceratops' eyes. "What are its symptoms?" she asked Dr. Harding.

"Trouble breathing. Trouble walking," he answered.

Alan and Ellie talked to the doctor for a while. Then Ellie walked into the open field, searching for an answer. Minutes later she came back to the group. The three doctors stood together, thinking.

"She must be sick from eating those berry plants in the field," Ellie finally said. "They could be poisonous."

Alan shook his head. "But Triceratops was a constant browser. And constant browsers would always be sick—not sick every six weeks. Something doesn't add up."

Tim, meanwhile, had wandered behind the dinosaur. He noticed a pile of smooth rocks on the ground by the Trike. Picking one up, he stared at it curiously.

"These look kind of familiar," he called out shyly. He hated to interrupt the doctors. "I've seen pictures of them."

"Where?" said Alan, not really paying attention.

Tim was just a kid, after all.

"Um—in your book."

Still, Alan ignored him. But Ellie joined Tim and peered at the stones. Suddenly her eyes lit up. She knew the answer!

"Gizzard stones!" she said.

Alan rushed over, excited. "That's it!" he cried.

"What do you mean?" Tim was confused.

"It's very simple," Ellie explained. "Some animals that don't have teeth—"

"—like birds," Alan continued. Just like before, they were finishing each other's sentences. "What some of them do is swallow rocks. They keep them in a sac in their stomachs—"

"—called a gizzard," said Ellie, taking over. "The gizzard helps them mash their food, and what happens—"

"—is after six weeks," Alan said, "the rocks get worn smooth. So the animal regurgitates them—"

". . . barfs them up," Ellie added, for Tim's benefit.

". . . and swallows fresh ones."

"And when this Triceratops did," Ellie finished triumphantly, "it swallowed poisonous berries and got sick. Good work, Tim."

Alan grunted.

Just then Gennaro broke into the conversation. "Doctors, if you please. I have to insist we get moving."

The sky was even darker now. Thunder rumbled. Whoosh! A strong wind swept through the trees.

"I'd like to stay with Dr. Harding," Ellie said, "and spend more time with the Trike."

"Sure," said Dr. Harding. "I've got a gas-powered vehicle. I can drop her off at the Visitor's Center before I take the boat out of here."

Lightning flashed. Gennaro was already pushing Tim and Lex back to the cars, while Ian Malcolm trailed behind.

"Go ahead, Alan," Ellie said as large drops of rain began to fall.

Alan felt strange leaving Ellie. He had a feeling that

something would go wrong. But Ellie was determined to stay, so he followed the others. A minute later, he raised his hand to wave, but Ellie wasn't looking. Then Ellie had the same idea. She waved to Alan. But it was too late. Alan had his back turned and was already up the hill.

Ellie sighed. It didn't really matter, she thought. They'd be together in just a little while. What could happen?

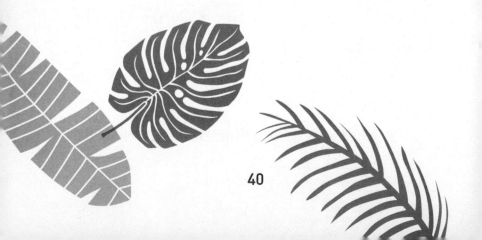

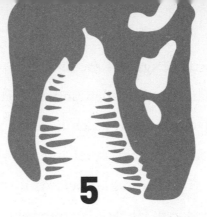

5

Mr. Hammond was still watching the video screens. "Good," he said. "They're in the cars again." The rain was coming down in driving sheets now.

"I'm turning the cars around," Ray Arnold said to him. "They're coming back."

Dennis Nedry stood and pretended to stretch. "Anybody want a Coke?" he asked. Everyone shook their heads, too busy to pay attention. Nedry grabbed the fake shaving can and took a step toward the door. Then he turned, as if he had just remembered something.

"Oh, I had to debug a few things in the computer.

One or two little systems might be off."

Mr. Hammond nodded absently. He wasn't even looking at Nedry. Nedry saw his chance. Quickly, he reached back to the computer and pressed EXECUTE.

Now he had one minute before the security systems would shut down. He raced to the specimen room. Just as he approached the door, the security lock clicked off. Perfect timing! The door swung open, and Nedry hurried inside. He saw a rack of glass slides. They were tagged APATOSAURUS, TYRANNOSAURUS, STEGOSAURUS, and so on. Nedry found just what he was looking for.

Ray Arnold sat at his computer, looking confused. On the screen, red lights were blinking one by one.

"That's odd," he said to Mr. Hammond. "Door security systems are shutting down."

"Well, Nedry said a few systems would go offline, didn't he?" Mr. Hammond said calmly.

Arnold kept staring at his computer screen. Blue lines started to flicker off, too.

"Now fences are failing," he called out urgently.

Then, "The phones are out."

Pffft! Suddenly all the video screens in the control room went black.

"Power is out everywhere!" Arnold shouted. "A few little systems? Ha!"

In a panic, Arnold raced over to Nedry's computer. He punched one button after another. He couldn't change the screen. Nedry had jammed the computer! He was the only person who could turn everything back on.

"The electric cars must have stopped, too," said Mr. Hammond, beginning to look concerned. "But where?"

Tim and Alexis sat with Gennaro in one car. Alan and Ian Malcolm were in the other. They were right outside the Tyrannosaurus paddock.

"Gennaro said to sit tight," Alan told Ian. He'd just come back from the other car and was soaking wet.

"Their power is out, too. Nothing to worry about. Probably just a little hiccup in the system."

All they could do was wait. In the front car, Tim and Lex were getting bored. The rain drummed on the roof. It was driving Tim crazy. He felt like they'd been there for hours.

"I think Mr. Grant is really . . . smart," Lex said dreamily. She thought he was cute, too. But she'd never say that to her brother. Besides, he was staring out the window—ignoring her as usual.

"Did you feel that?" Tim asked. At first Lex didn't know what he was talking about. But then she felt it, also. The car was shaking.

There were loud quaking sounds and it seemed as though the earth was moving—like something was taking giant footsteps.

Gennaro's eyes widened in fear. The sound got louder. The vibrations felt stronger. Whatever it was, it was coming closer. And then they all saw it. Tyrannosaurus rex. It was gripping the fence. Gennaro stared in horror. Oh no, he thought. The dinosaur should have felt an electric shock. The power must be out in the fences, too! But would it break through?

The T. rex swung its mighty head. Tim gasped. Its boxy head was bigger than Tim's whole body. And its body was bigger than a bus. The dinosaur waved its short, silly-looking arms in the air. Then it clawed the fence. The Tyrannosaurus was tearing it down!

All at once Gennaro bolted out of the car. He didn't say a word. He just ran, leaving Tim and Lex all alone. Lex began to scream. But Gennaro didn't stop. He raced toward a small building a short distance down the road. Moments later, he reached it and ran inside. But the building wasn't finished yet. Gennaro couldn't lock the wooden door behind him.

"What's he doing?" Ian asked Alan. They hadn't noticed the Tyrannosaurus yet.

Then they saw the fence come down. The Tyrannosaurus was free! It stood on the park road, eyeing the two cars.

"Don't move," Alan whispered to Ian. "It can't see us if we don't move."

The T. rex bent down. It peered through the car window at Ian. Ian froze. He couldn't have moved if he'd wanted to.

Suddenly the first car lit up like a beacon. Lex had turned on a flashlight. The dinosaur raised its head. It was drawn to the light.

"I'm sorry, sorry, sorry," Lex mumbled to Tim as the T. rex thudded closer. It lifted its head high. Tim and Lex could see it through the sunroof.

Roar! The dinosaur opened its mouth wide. It roared again. It was so loud, the car windows rattled.

Then the T. rex struck.

6

The dinosaur lifted its powerful leg. Smash! It kicked the car. Windows shattered, and the car tilted on its side. The dinosaur lowered its head and butted the car off the rail.

Inside, Tim and Lex tumbled about as the car rolled over. Now it was upside down. Tim twisted around to look out the window. They were right by a cliff.

The T. rex towered over the car. It put one leg on the frame and tore at the undercarriage of the car with its jaws. Biting at anything it could get ahold of, it ripped the rear axle free, tossed it aside, and bit a tire. Lex and Tim were trapped. And the dinosaur was about to push them over the cliff!

Alan couldn't stand it anymore. He had to do something! Jumping out of his car, he shouted, "Hey! Over here!" The dinosaur dropped the car and turned toward him. Alan waited to get its complete attention. Then he threw a flare over the cliff. The Tyrannosaurus lunged after it, but stopped inches from the edge.

Ian Malcolm watched from the car. In a flash, he leaped out of the car, too. Quickly, he ran for the building. But he caught the dinosaur's eye and the T. rex whirled around. As it did, its tail snapped behind it, striking Alan.

Alan went flying. But the dinosaur only noticed Ian. It gave chase, bending close to the ground. Then, with one flick of its head, it nudged Ian from behind. The dinosaur didn't use much of its strength. Still, Ian sailed through the air and smashed through a wood portion of the wall and into the building.

Inside, Gennaro was cowering in a corner, next to a toilet. He was in a bathroom! Suddenly the

Tyrannosaurus's head broke through the wall. Wood chips and cement pieces flew everywhere. Crash! The roof collapsed. Ian and Gennaro were buried in the rubble.

Slowly Alan got to his feet. He watched the T. rex nose around the fallen building. Then he saw it stop. It had found something. Alan couldn't bear to watch. He turned away as Gennaro screamed.

There was nothing Alan could do to save him. And Ian was probably a goner, too, he thought. But he could try to help the kids. He scrambled over to the smashed-up car. Reaching in through a broken window, he pulled out Lex.

"Tim's knocked out," she told him.

Boom! A giant T. rex foot landed right in front of them. Alan and Lex stood still as statues. There was nowhere to go. They were caught between the dinosaur and the cliff. The dinosaur bent down, inches away from them. Then, once again, it pushed the car.

Tim opened his eyes. He saw one giant eye staring

at him through the open hole of the sunroof. He screamed, and that seemed to fascinate the dinosaur. It stretched its long tongue through the hole. It was trying to wrap its tongue around Tim!

Tim wedged himself tightly into the seat. He was just out of the dinosaur's reach. Roaring in defeat, the T. rex lunged again. The car shifted, then began to roll. It was heading toward the cliff, gathering speed. And Lex and Alan were right in front of it!

Alan grabbed Lex and swung her onto his back. Then he began to climb down the cliff. Seconds later, the car went over. Whizz! Alan pressed up against the cliffside. The car just missed them.

"Timmy!" cried Lex as the car dropped through the air. Crash! It landed in a treetop—and hung there in the branches.

The Tyrannosaurus gave one last roar. But everyone was beyond its reach. It turned away, leaving them alone. For now.

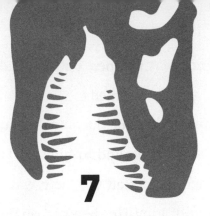

7

Dennis Nedry jumped into a truck. He had to hurry if he was going to make that boat. Clutching the shaving cream can full of dinosaur specimens, he drove through the park gates. A moment later he came to another gate. This one said DANGER! ELECTRIFIED FENCE! THIS DOOR CANNOT BE OPENED WHEN FENCE IS ARMED! But Nedry knew the fence was turned off. He reached over and pushed it open. Then he raced toward the docks, driving deeper into the park.

The rain beat against the vehicle. It was coming down so hard, Nedry could barely see. He stepped on the gas. Time was running out. He had to get to the ship!

Ten minutes passed. "I should have been there by now," Nedry muttered to himself. He checked his watch. When he looked up, there was a cement wall right in front of him! He slammed on the brakes.

The truck skidded off the road, landing in a muddy ditch. Nedry put the truck in reverse. The tires spun, but the vehicle didn't move. It was stuck. Nedry sighed as he got out. He'd have to push.

Hoot, hoot! A soft noise came from the woods. Was it an owl? Nedry shined his flashlight into the trees. There was nothing there. Hoot, hoot! Nedry froze. This time he saw something. And it wasn't an owl.

It was a dinosaur. Nedry peered at it through the rain. He didn't think it looked dangerous. Only four feet tall, it was spotted and had a bright crest on its head. *And* it was hopping around like a kangaroo. Nedry almost laughed. He didn't know it was a Dilophosaurus—the dinosaur with the poisonous spit.

"Nice boy," said Nedry. "Now run along. I have to move the truck."

The dinosaur didn't listen. It circled Nedry playfully. Hoot, hoot! it called. It was acting like it wanted to play. But it was getting in Nedry's way.

"Go on!" said Nedry. "Go home! Dinnertime! Aren't you hungry?"

The dinosaur just stared at him.

Nedry spied a stick on the ground. Picking it up, he shouted, "Fetch!" Then he tossed it behind a tree.

The Dilophosaurus leaped behind the tree. But a second later it was back. Hoot! it called, jumping right in front of Nedry. Nedry was so startled, he fell backward. He didn't feel like laughing now. He was angry.

"I said, beat it!" Nedry picked up a rock and threw it at the dinosaur.

The Dilophosaurus hooted softly. It sounded sad, almost as if its feelings were hurt. Then it hopped away.

Finally, Nedry set to work on the truck. He almost

had it out of the ditch when he heard the hooting again. The Dilophosaurus was standing a few feet away. Suddenly, it reared back its head, then snapped it forward. Splat! A big glob of spit smacked Nedry in the chest. Splat! Another glob hit him in the face.

"Ahh!" screamed Nedry. The first shot had just felt strange. But the spit that hit his face seeped into his eyes. Nedry felt a shooting pain there. An incredible shooting pain. A second passed, and Nedry realized he couldn't see. He was blind! Feeling his way around, he stumbled into the truck. He sat, clutching his eyes in pain. Then he heard a hissing noise. The Dilophosaurus was in the vehicle, too! Nedry shrieked in horror. But no one could help him now.

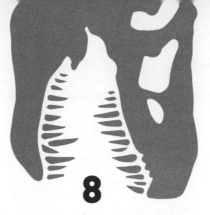

8

On the other side of the park, Alan and Lex had managed to scramble down the cliff. It had stopped raining, and they were looking up at the tree. The car was still stuck in the branches. But it didn't look very secure. A branch broke. The car fell a few feet. Then it stopped, held up by more branches.

Lex was shaking. She could barely breathe. Her brother was up there! Please let Timmy be okay. Please let Timmy be okay, she kept saying to herself.

"I have to go help your brother," Alan said. Lex shook even more. She didn't want to be left alone. Gennaro had left them alone, and look what happened.

Alan wanted to comfort her. But he didn't know how. Feeling clumsy, he patted her on the head. Lex threw her arms around his waist and wouldn't let go. Alan looked around. A large drainpipe ran along the ground. He led Lex over to it.

"Shh, shh. I'll take care of you," he told her. "I'm not going to leave. Just stay here for a few minutes while I help Tim. You'll be okay."

Alan coaxed Lex a bit more, and finally she crawled into the pipe.

Alan made sure Lex was safely inside; then he walked back to the tree. He took a breath and began to climb. Up, up, up. The tree seemed unbelievably tall, but at last he reached the car. Carefully, Alan opened the driver's door. Tim was huddled on the other side, hugging his knees. His face was streaked with blood and tears. He looked so frightened! Alan's heart went out to him.

"I threw up," said Tim, ashamed.

"That's okay. Just give me your hand."

Tim didn't move.

"Come on, Tim. I won't tell anyone you threw up. Now please give me your hand."

Tim reached out. But just as Alan got hold of him, the car lurched and Tim tumbled out the door. He fell against Alan, and they both dropped down a few branches. They were right below the car. Suddenly they heard a groan—the branch that held the car was giving way!

"Let's go!" said Alan.

Together, they half climbed, half fell down the tree. Snap! Snap! More branches broke. The car was falling. It was heading right for them!

They jumped. Alan and Tim hit the ground—hard. But the car was almost on top of them, so Alan grabbed Tim and rolled to the side. A second later the car landed—right where they had been. The car stood upright, its roof inches from Alan and Tim. Then it tipped over. . . .

Tim squeezed his eyes shut. After all that, the car

was still going to fall on them! Thud! Tim felt a rush of air. But that was all. How strange, he thought, opening his eyes. He realized he was inside the car. They'd been saved by the hole in the sunroof.

Alan brought Tim over to the drainpipe where Lex was hiding. Then he peered inside. Lex was curled into a ball, shaking with fright. She was too terrified to crawl back out.

"Come on, Lex," Alan said in a soothing voice. "Hiding isn't the answer. We have to get moving and improve our situation."

Lex just stared at him, not budging an inch. Tim rolled his eyes. Lex could be so ridiculous!

Alan tried again. "Tim's out here. He's okay."

Still there was no response.

Then Alan tried something else. "Of course you could just wait in there while we go back and get help."

"Yeah," Tim said quickly. "Let's go."

"You'll probably be safe alone," Alan went on. "But I couldn't say for sure."

"You're a liar!" shouted Lex. "You said you wouldn't leave me."

"I'm using psychology on you," said Alan. Lex just kept staring at him. Didn't he know things like psychology never work?

Alan took a deep breath. "Okay. We're going to walk back. Together. But we won't go near the road. The T. rex probably staked that out as a feeding range. That means this whole paddock is empty. It's safe. So we'll walk through here. What do you say?"

In answer, Lex crawled out of the pipe. Alan sounded so sure of himself. He made everything seem okay. But as they began to walk, Alan made a mistake: he kept talking.

"It might be a little slow going. But it can't be more than three or four miles to the Visitor's Center. Maybe the T. rex is done feeding. No, no. Let's not kid ourselves. A carnivore can eat twenty-five percent of its weight in just one sitting. So really, it's probably just up to the main course and—"

Alan stopped in midsentence. Both kids were in the drainpipe now.

Back at the control room, Mr. Hammond, Ray Arnold, Robert Muldoon, and Ellie, who had gotten a ride back from Dr. Harding, had realized that Nedry was gone for good. Without him, they couldn't turn the power back on. So there was nothing else to do. They had to go into the jungle and search for the others.

Now Ellie and Muldoon were driving down the dark park road.

"Hurry, hurry, hurry," Ellie said to Muldoon. She had a feeling that something terrible had happened. At last they came to the broken Tyrannosaurus fence.

"Oh no!" cried Ellie. Things looked worse than she'd imagined. One electric car was gone. The other was empty, its doors hanging open. Muldoon ran over to the wrecked building. Then he saw Gennaro's body and stopped short.

Roar! They could hear the Tyrannosaurus in the distance. Ellie joined Muldoon, frightened.

"The T. rex could be anywhere," Muldoon said to her. They heard another sound nearby, but this one was human. It sounded like a moan.

"It's Malcolm!" Muldoon cried. Ian Malcolm was half buried under the rubble. He was alive but in bad shape. He was barely conscious, and one leg was covered with blood.

Roar! The Tyrannosaurus was closer now.

"Can we risk moving him?" Ellie asked.

"Please. Risk it," Malcolm croaked.

Carefully, they carried him to the backseat of the truck. Then Ellie went back to the empty electric car. She wouldn't give up! Desperately, she looked for clues. What could have happened? "Look!" she said. There were three sets of footprints. Alan and the kids were alive!

ROAR! The Tyrannosaurus was getting closer. The earth shook with each thundering step. The booming noise grew louder—and faster.

Still, Ellie couldn't leave the spot. Maybe Alan was nearby. She had to find him! Suddenly the charging Tyrannosaurus burst onto the road!

"Come on!" shouted Ian with all his might.

Ellie leaped into the truck. Muldoon was already behind the wheel. He hit the gas, and they were off. But the vehicle was slow to pick up speed. And the Tyrannosaurus was coming after them—fast! Ellie looked back. It was closing the gap!

The vehicle smashed through branches and careened over rocks. Finally it picked up speed. The T. rex fell behind, then faded from sight.

For a few moments, they drove in silence. Then Ian gave a little laugh.

"Think they'll have that on the tour?" he asked.

9

Alan had finally convinced Lex and Tim to come out of the drainpipe. And now, slowly but surely, they were making their way through Jurassic Park. A full moon lit the jungle, so they were able to see. The strange light made everything look spooky. But they didn't have a choice—they had to keep going. They had to get to the Visitor's Center. So Alan, Lex, and Tim hiked and climbed through the night, always on the lookout for dinosaurs.

There was no power anywhere in the park. That meant the dinosaurs were still on the loose . . . including the T. rex.

Alan checked a map he'd taken from the Visitor's Center. Was that only this morning? It seemed like they'd been walking for a million years.

"Looks like we're heading west," he said. "That's good, I think. We should definitely hit the Visitor's Center this way."

Lex took his hand. They walked side by side for a moment. Then Alan turned to Tim. "You want to hold my other hand?" he asked.

Tim just shook his head. He was determined to make it on his own.

"He'll never hold anybody's hand," said Lex. "Timmy is a dinosaur. A jerkosaurus."

"Straight A–brainiac," Tim shot back.

"Dorkatops!"

Roar! The sound silenced everyone.

"You both look pretty tired. I think we should find someplace to rest," Alan said.

ROAR!

"Now!"

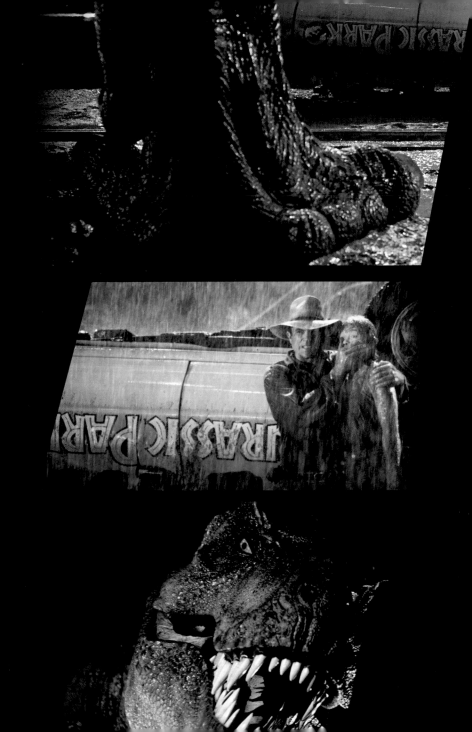

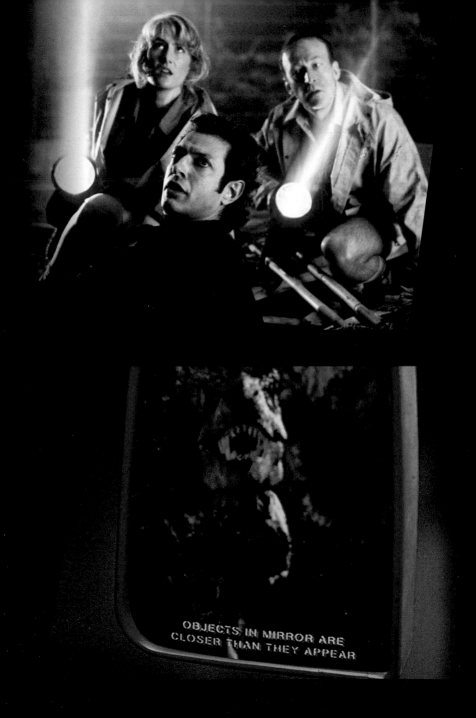

OBJECTS IN MIRROR ARE
CLOSER THAN THEY APPEAR

Once again, Alan climbed a tree. But this time, Tim and Lex were right behind him. When they reached the top, they were awestruck by the view. The park stretched for miles around. The trees, the meadows, the herds of dinosaurs—it was all a beautiful sight. Lex thought it was romantic, too.

"Are you and Dr. Sattler married?" Lex asked, settling in the branches.

"Well, we're . . ."

"Those are brachiosaurs," Tim said, trying to change the subject. He pointed out the dozens of plant-eating dinosaurs. Their long, graceful necks towered above the trees.

"Yes, they are brachiosaurs," Alan told him. "It's a great name. It means 'arm lizard.' "

Lex leaned forward. "Don't listen to him," she said to Alan. "Timmy always talks about dinosaurs when he thinks something is mushy."

"That's okay," said Alan. "So do I."

Tim thought they should go back to talking about dinosaurs. He had a question. "How could dinosaurs turn into birds? Birds don't have teeth and some dinosaurs do."

"Simple evolution," explained Alan. "As birds evolved, they lost their teeth. They began to use gizzard stones instead, like the Triceratops."

"Yeah, but . . ." Tim was excited. He thought he could outsmart Alan. "But shouldn't there be a missing link? After the dinosaurs disappeared, shouldn't there have been birds with teeth?"

"There were," Alan answered. "Toothed seabirds. They were found in Kansas in the 1800s."

Tim thought about that for a second. Satisfied, he stopped his questioning and the three fell silent. They could hear the animals calling each other. Some calls sounded just like music. Alan smiled at the pretty sounds. But after a moment, his smile faded. Were those mating calls? he wondered. And how could that be? All the dinosaurs were supposed to be female.

His thoughts were interrupted by Lex. "What if the dinosaurs come while we're sleeping?"

"I'll stay awake," Alan promised. Lex came closer and crawled under his arm. Tim hesitated for a second, then curled under Alan's other arm. Tim and Lex leaned back against the tree trunk. Minutes later they were fast asleep.

Alan looked down at the sleeping kids. Who would have thought that he'd be sitting here with two children under his arms? He sighed. Maybe kids weren't so terrible after all. He just hoped he wouldn't let them down.

The next morning, Alan and the kids woke with a start. A Brachiosaurus was munching on leaves—right by their heads. Lex opened her mouth to scream, but nothing came out.

"It's okay," said Tim. "It's a Brachiosaurus, Lex.

A veggiesaurus."

He climbed up to a higher branch so he could pat the dinosaur's head. Alan, meanwhile, was inspecting its mouth. The dinosaur didn't seem to mind. It just continued munching. Feeling a little braver, Lex edged closer. She was just in front of the dinosaur's head. She reached out, gently patting its nose.

Achoo! The dinosaur sneezed. But it was more like an explosion.

"Eew!" said Lex in disgust. She was dripping wet from head to toe.

Lex dropped to the ground and stomped away.

"Oh, great," Tim said to Alan as they climbed down, too. "Now she'll never try anything again. She'll just sit in her room with her computer for the rest of her life."

Alan jumped the last few feet. Then he saw something that made him stop in his tracks. "Oh my," he said in surprise. He crouched down and picked it up. Tim landed next to him, and Lex came over, too.

"What is it?" asked Tim. Alan was holding a thin piece of white shell.

"It's a dinosaur egg," Alan said. Part of him couldn't believe it. But another part wasn't surprised at all. "The dinosaurs are breeding." Right in front of him was a whole group of eggs that were already hatched.

"But my grandpa said all the dinosaurs are girls!" exclaimed Tim.

"He also said scientists changed the dinosaurs' genetic code. They blended it with frog DNA," Alan explained. "And some West African frogs can change sex when there are only male or females around. That way they're able to breed." Alan shook his head. Ian was right. Life found a way.

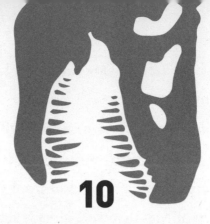

10

The sun was just coming up, and Ian, Ellie, and Muldoon were safely back at the control room. Ray Arnold was hunched over his computer, where he'd been all night. No matter what he tried, he couldn't fix the security systems. Dennis Nedry's commands were too complicated.

"I can't get Jurassic Park back online," he finally admitted to Mr. Hammond.

"We'll have to shut down the entire system," Mr. Hammond said. "That will wipe out everything Nedry did. Then we can turn everything back on. The systems will be back to normal. The fences, the phones—

everything will be working. And then we can locate Alan and my grandkids."

Ellie, Muldoon, and Ian listened closely. Shutting down the system would turn *everything* off. No lights. No computers. And what if the system didn't come back on? Then they'd really be sunk. There'd be no chance of survival at all.

Ray Arnold hated to do it. But he also knew he had no choice. He walked over to a red metal box on a wall. He took a key from his belt and unlocked the panel.

Inside was a row of switches. One by one, Ray Arnold flipped them off. "You asked for it," he said. And he pulled the final switch.

Every computer and every light shut off. They were in near darkness. Seconds ticked by. Then Arnold flipped the switches back on. Nothing happened.

For a moment Arnold was too panicked to move. Then he raced over to the main computer. "It's okay!" he shouted. The screen was glowing. A minute later two words appeared: SYSTEM READY.

71

"But the lights are still out," said Ian, confused.

"The shutdown turned off the circuit breakers," Arnold explained. "We just have to turn them back on. Then all the systems will come back. The circuit box is in the maintenance shed. That's on the other side of the main compound. I'll go. In three minutes, the entire park will be under control."

Arnold hurried out of the control room. Ellie and the others followed, carrying Ian on a stretcher. They were going to an underground shelter across from the Visitor's Center.

"Muldoon," Mr. Hammond ordered. "Round up any staff members who are still on the island and bring them over, too."

Mr. Hammond thought everyone would be safer in the shelter. But even he knew it wasn't dinosaur-proof.

All morning long, Alan, Tim, and Lex tramped through the jungle. At last Alan let them rest.

"The Visitor's Center should be just a mile from here. If we—" Alan stopped talking. A strange animal cry echoed through the jungle. Then the ground began to shake. Alan, squinting into the distance, could only make out shapes. But the shapes were coming closer. And seconds later, Alan realized what was happening. Dozens of dinosaurs were running. It was a stampede!

"They're just like a flock of birds," said Alan, "running away from an enemy!"

Then they heard another cry. ROAR! It was the Tyrannosaurus. But where was it? The sound seemed to come from everywhere at once.

Suddenly the dinosaur herd changed direction. Now it was heading straight for Alan, Tim, and Lex!

Quickly they ran for the cover of the jungle. But the dinosaurs began to run faster and faster. Alan knew they'd never make it. He pulled the kids under a mass of giant tree roots. They hid just in time. A second later, the herd thundered above their heads. They could see clawed feet through the roots. The dinosaurs were running for the jungle.

ROAR! The T. rex burst out from behind the trees. It had been in the jungle all along! And now it stood in front of the herd.

The dinosaurs scattered. But the Tyrannosaurus was already on top of them. With a mighty roar it sank its teeth into the closest dinosaur.

Tim and Alan watched, fascinated. But Lex knew this was the time to leave—while the T. rex was busy. "Come on, you guys!" she said.

They ran toward the Visitor's Center.

The underground shelter was hot and crowded. And, like the rest of the park, it was unfinished. Ellie paced back and forth as best she could among crates and ladders. She was waiting with Mr. Hammond, Ian, Muldoon, and the other Jurassic Park employees for Ray Arnold to return.

"Something went wrong," she said after a while.

"I'm going to get the power back on."

"I'll ride shotgun," offered Muldoon.

Everyone sprang into action. Muldoon hurried over to a steel cabinet. Inside were various guns, rockets, and other weapons. Muldoon took the biggest gun he could find and quickly loaded it with bullets. In another corner of the shelter, Mr. Hammond unearthed a set of blueprints. He pulled out a map of the maintenance shed. Then, with Ian at his side, he pored over it inch by inch, trying to find the circuit box. Meanwhile, Ellie grabbed a flashlight from an open crate. Right next to it was a walkie-talkie set. She tossed one to Mr. Hammond.

"Think you can read that map and talk us through the shed?" she asked.

"Absolutely," he said.

Seconds later, they were ready.

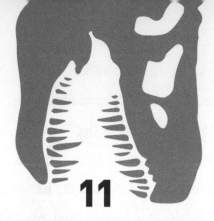

11

Alan, Lex, and Tim trudged down the last hill before the Visitor's Center. They were exhausted. And there, right in front of them, was an incredibly high fence. It was the fence that protected the main compound. They were so close, but so tired. Tim and Lex collapsed on the ground.

"Power's still out," Alan said, poking the fence with a stick. "It's a big climb, though. Think you can make it?"

"Nope," said Tim.

"Way too high," said Lex.

The Tyrannosaurus roared in the distance. Tim and Lex leaped to their feet, ready to climb.

To get to the maintenance shed, Ellie and Muldoon had to cross the compound. That meant skirting the jungle—and walking past the Raptor pen. They stepped onto the path.

"Keep moving," Muldoon whispered as they approached the pen.

Ellie kept walking. But as she drew close to the Raptor pen, her heart beat faster. She looked at the fence that surrounded it.

"Oh God," she said.

There was a hole in the fence. A hole large enough for an animal to slip through. And Ellie knew what that meant. The Raptors were out!

Then Ellie saw the shed. "We can make it if we run," she said.

"No, we can't. We're being hunted." Muldoon

nodded toward the jungle.

Ellie saw the shadow of an animal creeping through the palm trees. It was a Raptor.

"Run to the shed," Muldoon ordered, raising his rifle. "I'll take care of it."

Ellie hopped over branches. She sprinted across open spaces. She didn't look back. At last she was there. She threw open the door and slammed it behind her.

"I'm in," Ellie said, speaking into the walkie-talkie.

"Okay," Mr. Hammond answered. He and Ian began to direct her: down a metal staircase and through a passageway, until she reached a big metal box. Ellie found it. Then, listening to Mr. Hammond, she opened the door. Inside was a handle. Ellie pumped it. Next she pressed a series of buttons.

"The buttons turn on the park systems," Mr. Hammond was saying. "Activate them all!"

The last one was marked COMPOUND FENCE.

Alan climbed the fence faster than the kids. He was already on the ground when he saw the warning light flash on a fence post. The power was about to go on. And Lex and Tim were at the top!

"Get off the fence," Alan shouted. "Now!"

Quickly Lex scrambled down. But Tim froze with fear. He was too terrified to climb down. The light flashed quicker and quicker.

"Let go, Tim!" Alan cried.

Suddenly there was a loud buzz. The fence hummed as a current ran through it. It was electrified!

Tim shook violently. Then he was thrown to the ground.

Alan and Lex raced over. Tim's face was white. His hands were burned a bright red. But worst of all, he wasn't breathing.

"Oh no! He's dead! He's dead!" Lex cried out.

Alan ripped Tim's shirt open. He pressed down on his chest, performing CPR. "Come on, Timmy," he said. Then he breathed into Tim's mouth.

"Ahhh!" Tim gasped as he came to.

"Timmy!" Lex shouted happily. He was still in a daze. But he was going to be all right. Alan carefully wrapped Tim's hands with pieces of his shirt. Then he and Lex helped Tim over to the Visitor's Center.

Lights flickered on in the maintenance shed, and Ellie blinked in the sudden brightness. Then she saw the Raptor.

It was behind the circuit box. For a second, it just looked at her. Then it slashed out. Ellie stepped back just in time. But now something was brushing her shoulder. It was an arm—Ray Arnold's arm. He was dead, stuck behind a tangle of pipes. Ellie didn't stay for a closer look. The Raptor was about to spring.

She took off, running down the passageway. But the Raptor was close behind. She could hear its sharp claws clicking against the floor. It drew closer . . . and closer. When Ellie reached the door, she was just one step ahead of the Raptor. Flinging the door open, she spun around and slammed it shut. Ellie took a deep breath. She was outside. Better yet, the Raptor was inside. Trapped.

Muldoon stole quietly through the jungle. He could barely see the gray Raptor through the leaves. But the Raptor was moving deeper into the jungle. And so was Muldoon.

Suddenly the Raptor stopped. It rose to its full height.

"Gotcha!" said Muldoon, about to pull the trigger.

Then he paused. The Raptor was the perfect target. Too perfect. Was this a setup? Those were Muldoon's last thoughts.

Another Raptor pounced from behind.

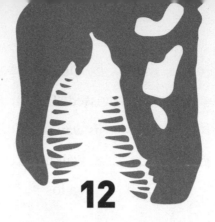

12

The Visitor's Center was deserted. Chairs were turned over. Signs were on the floor. Branches poked through the windows. It looked like the jungle had taken over.

Alan led Lex and Tim into the restaurant.

"I need to find the others," he said. "And Tim needs a doctor. Will you take care of him for me, Lex?"

Lex nodded, her eyes wide. She was terrified.

Tim's hair was wild from the shock of electricity. Alan looked at him a moment. Then he smoothed it down.

"Big Tim, the human piece of toast," he said softly.

Tim gave a weak laugh. Quickly, before he could change his mind, Alan kissed Tim and Lex on the foreheads. Then he made his way across the restaurant.

"Be right back," he said, walking out the door.

For a moment, Lex was at a loss. What should they do next?

"Are you hungry, Timmy?" She went to the food counter and started loading things onto a tray. Suddenly she froze.

"Something's here," she whispered. Through the restaurant window they could see into the lobby. There was a life-size picture of a Raptor. And right next to it was a real one!

"Can you run, Tim?" she asked.

"I don't think so," he answered faintly.

Lex pulled Tim to his feet. Throwing his arm over her shoulder, she helped him to the kitchen. As quietly as she could, she shut the shiny metal door. There was no lock. Then she led Tim down an aisle to the back of the room. They tried to hide behind a counter.

All at once they saw the Raptor's head. It was peering at them through the round window of the kitchen door. Bang! The Raptor thumped against the metal. The door didn't budge.

The Raptor looked at the door handle. It was figuring out how it worked! Slowly, it reached out its clawed hand. Inside the kitchen, Lex and Tim stared. The handle was turning.

The door opened.

The Raptor stood framed in the doorway. Drawing itself up to its full height, it snarled. Then it moved into the room. But it wasn't alone. Right behind it was another Raptor. They both paused, sniffing the air.

The first Raptor went down one aisle. The other Raptor chose a different one. Tim and Lex crawled down the third aisle—the center one—in the opposite direction. They were heading for the door. But first, they had to get past the Raptors. And ordinary kitchen counters were the only things between Lex and Tim, and the dinosaurs.

Tim and Lex moved toward the door. Just as they passed the Raptors, one of the dinosaurs turned and knocked pots and pans off the counter—right on the kids' heads. Somehow, Tim and Lex managed to keep quiet. Lex kept crawling, but Tim was falling behind—and Lex didn't realize it.

Exhausted, Tim brushed up against some pots and they clattered to the ground. Hearing the noise, the Raptors stopped. Then they turned and headed for Tim.

Click, click. Suddenly there was another noise. It was coming from the other end of the aisle. The Raptors turned again. It was Lex, tapping a spoon on the floor. They began to move toward her. Quickly Lex slid into a steel cabinet. She tried to pull down the shiny sliding door, but it was stuck. And the Raptors were coming closer.

Tim, meanwhile, spotted a walk-in freezer. If he could just get inside! Using all his strength, he pulled himself up. Then he limped toward the freezer. But one Raptor saw Tim moving and headed his way.

Now one Raptor was closing in on Lex, the other on Timmy.

The Raptors pounced at the same time. But instead of striking Lex, the Raptor went for her reflection on a shiny cabinet door. Thud! It hit the cabinet hard and fell to the ground.

Tim made it to the freezer. He ripped the door open and stumbled inside. The floor was icy. So icy, Tim went sliding across the floor. The Raptor was just behind him and skidded, too—right past Tim.

There was a moment of confusion in the freezer and Tim saw his chance to escape. He hurried out the door, the Raptor at his heels. Slam! Lex flung the door closed just in time. The Raptor was trapped inside.

Lex looked at the other Raptor. It was getting to its feet. She threw her arm around Tim, and together they raced into the hallway. Suddenly dark shapes loomed in front of them. But they couldn't stop running. Crash! They careened into the figures and fell to the ground.

A second later they were yanked to their feet.

It was Alan and Ellie.

"Let's go!" said Alan.

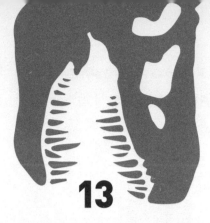

13

Alan, Ellie, Lex, and Tim raced to the control room. Alan made sure Tim was okay. Then he ran back to lock the door.

"Hey. The door doesn't lock," Alan said. "The computer has to give the signal."

Ellie was studying the flashing computer screen. "We have to turn on the programs," she explained.

Bang! A snarling Raptor hit the door. Alan pushed back, trying to keep it out. Bang! The Raptor tried again. The door gave way—a little. Alan couldn't hold it by himself. Ellie ran over to help. But even two people couldn't keep it shut for long.

Lex slid into the command chair at the computer. Her fingers flew over the keyboard. Where was that door lock command? At last she found it. There was a beep, a buzz, and the lock clicked shut. The Raptor was locked outside.

Ellie joined Lex at the main computer. They put their heads together. Minutes later, they had all the park systems running. At last! Jurassic Park was under control. Meanwhile, Alan phoned the underground shelter.

"The kids are fine," he told Mr. Hammond. "And we've got everything back on. You can call the mainland for help."

Suddenly there was a scream and Alan dropped the phone. The Raptor was at the window.

"Quick!" said Alan. "The ceiling." He ushered everyone up a ladder and Ellie moved aside a ceiling panel.

Then she, Lex, and Tim pulled themselves up into the crawl space. Alan was about to follow when the Raptor hurled itself into the room, shattering the glass into little pieces. Without a moment to lose, Alan swung through the open panel. He caught up to the others and they ran across the ceiling—panel by panel—with Alan helping Tim along.

But the Raptor saw the ceiling move beneath them. It leapt up high, smashing through the panel in front of Ellie. For a second the Raptor hung suspended in air, snapping and snarling. Then it fell to the floor. Alan motioned everyone to keep moving.

Seconds later, the Raptor broke through the ceiling again. This time, it struck the panel Lex was on.

"Ahh!" she screamed.

Lex was lifted up, right on the Raptor's head! Alan kicked at its neck. It snapped back and dropped to the ground. Lex was falling, too. Just in time, Alan caught her by the shirt. She dangled for a second. Then Alan pulled her into the ceiling.

"Into the air duct!" Alan shouted.

Metal boomed all around as they raced through the

duct. They were safe for the moment. But they had to get down to escape. Finally they came to a metal grating above the Visitor's Center lobby. Looking down, they could see the dinosaur skeletons and the scaffolding.

"Let's go through here!" said Alan, lifting out the grating. Everyone dropped onto the scaffolding. It was too high to jump to the ground. There was only one thing to do.

Alan stepped onto the Brachiosaurus skeleton. Would it hold his weight? Yes, and it seemed strong enough to hold more. The anchor bolts in the ceiling were keeping the skeleton firmly in place.

"Come on," Alan said to the others. "It's okay."

Bone by bone, Ellie and the kids started to climb down the skeleton. All at once there was a groaning sound. The bolts were pulling free of the ceiling.

Ellie looked up. "We're going to make it," she said. "We're going to—"

Just then came the sound of claws running on metal, and the Raptor flew out of the air duct. It landed with a loud thump on the scaffolding above their heads. The Brachiosaurus swayed with the impact.

"Go, go!" shouted Alan. Everyone picked up speed, scampering down the skeleton at breakneck pace.

Making its move, the Raptor sprang onto the Brachiosaurus's neck. But the extra weight was too much. The anchor bolts ripped free, and the skeleton collapsed like a flimsy house of cards. Alan, Ellie, and the kids tumbled to the ground with the Raptor right behind. They landed on a pile of bones, the Raptor a few feet away.

Everyone was okay. But now the Raptor was trying to stand. It got up shakily, staggered for a moment, then fell back to the floor. Alan and Ellie gathered the kids close, helping them to their feet. The main entrance was just a few yards away. If they could get outside . . .

They were almost there when they saw the other Raptor. It was in the doorway, blocking their escape. Behind them the first Raptor pulled itself up. Hissing, the Raptors crouched for their attack. There was nowhere to hide, and nothing to do.

All of a sudden, a tremendous tearing noise echoed through the lobby. A dark, giant shadow fell across the room.

The Tyrannosaurus rex had broken through the lobby wall! Compared to the mighty T. rex, the Raptors looked like toys—vicious, hungry toys.

The T. rex lowered its great head, reaching down and down. Then it clamped its jaws around the nearest Raptor. The helpless dinosaur howled in pain as the T. rex lifted it high into the air. For a moment the Tyrannosaurus tossed its head back and forth, swinging the Raptor in its mouth. Finally it dropped the Raptor to the ground.

The Raptor howled with its final breath.

Then the lobby was silent, and Alan was able to hear the screech of tires. Mr. Hammond and Ian Malcolm had just pulled up in a truck. But the second Raptor was going into action. Leaping twelve feet into the air, it lunged at the T. rex. The Raptor clawed at the

T. rex's side, slashing out with its deadly-sharp claws. The Tyrannosaurus bellowed and began to fight back.

Alan didn't waste a second. He herded everyone outside and into the waiting truck—just as the T. rex felled the Raptor with one mighty blow. But before the vehicle could pull away, the T. rex whirled around to chase them. Luckily, its powerful tail struck the other skeleton—that of the Tyrannosaurus rex—and the living T. rex stopped in confusion. The skeleton crumpled, and Alan saw the Tyrannosaurus bones fall harmlessly around the living, breathing dinosaur.

Nothing can compare to the real thing, Alan thought. Nothing. And they sped away.

When they were a safe distance from the T. rex, Alan closed his eyes. He felt relief. Exhaustion. Everything at once. Then he looked around—at Ellie, Lex, and Tim—and had to grin.

"By the way, Mr. Hammond," he said. "I've given

this careful consideration. And I've decided not to endorse Jurassic Park."

Mr. Hammond smiled and said, "After careful consideration, so have I."

A little later they were on board a helicopter, heading for home. Rescue teams had been sent from the mainland, along with doctors who had examined each person. Ian Malcolm was going to be fine. So was Tim. They were safe. They were thankful. But they also felt a little sad. Jurassic Park would never open. The animals would have to be destroyed. Dinosaurs would never roam the earth again.

In the back of the helicopter, Alan sat with Lex and Tim. Ellie smiled at him. She never thought he'd be so comfortable with kids. He'd changed in the past couple of days. But then, she thought, they all had. They had made it out alive—they were survivors.

Ellie moved over to sit next to Alan. She grabbed

his hand and held it tight. Lex looked over. Quickly she reached for his other hand. She still thought he was cute.

Alan smiled at both of them. Then he gazed out the window. He saw a flock of birds fly by in perfect formation. They looked like a herd of dinosaurs, running across a field. Alan nudged Tim.

Tim looked out the window, too, then grinned. He understood. In some ways, dinosaurs would always live on.